Amanda the Anteater Stops Eating Ants

Matt Rufo

Illustrations by Kalpart

Strategic Book Publishing and Rights Co.

Strategic Book Publishing and Rights Co., LLC
USA | Singapore
www.sbpra.net

For information about special discounts for bulk purchases, please contact Strategic Book Publishing and Rights Co., LLC. Special Sales, at bookorder@sbpra.net.

ISBN: 978-1-68235-467-4

This book is dedicated to everyone who has ever had a dream in their life and thought they couldn't achieve it. Always believe in yourself and reach for the stars. No dream is out of reach when you work hard and believe in yourself. My daughter Samantha reminds me of this every day.

At about 8 a.m., Amanda the anteater was accustomed to awaken at almost the same time every day.

Amanda and all her anteater friends always awoke with ants as their most important agenda item of the day.

The ants anticipated the anteaters with animosity and they aggressively ran and hid.

As a typical day advanced for Amanda with the ants, alternative ideas entered her thoughts.

Amanda came across an avocado all alone on the ground. Imagine an anteater that ate something other than an ant!

It could be an amazing idea, but Amanda was afraid. What about all the other anteaters? Would they be angry? Amanda thought, *Today is the day!* and that avocado was all Amanda's.

The other anteaters halted and were filled with amazement as Amanda ate the avocado.

After that, she came across an apple, some asparagus, and a few almonds.

Other anteaters were against her outrageous acts, but Amanda decided to be her own anteater. In fact, she was not just an anteater anymore. She was Amanda.

Amanda decided from that day forward it was okay to explore new alternative ideas. Anything was possible for Amanda.

We'd like to know if you enjoyed the book.
Please consider leaving a review on the platform from which you purchased the book.

Practice makes perfect. Trace the lines for all your favorite letter A words:

AVOCADO,

APPLE,

ALMOND,

ANTEATER,

AMANDA,

ANT,

ANGRY,

AMAZING,
ANIMOSITY,
ANTICIPATED,
AWAKEN,
ACCUSTOMED,
AGENDA,
ALTERNATIVE

Have Amanda try to find her way through to an Avocado.

© Igor Zakowski | 123RF Stock Image

Practice drawing the letter A:

_____

_____

_____

_____

_____

_____

Practice drawing your best Anteater and like it on my Facebook page...

Author Matt Rufo

CPSIA information can be obtained
at www.ICGtesting.com
Printed in the USA
LVHW071620120821
695159LV00002B/43